A Templar Book

First published in the UK in 2015 by Templar Publishing,
part of the Bonnier Publishing Group,
Deepdene Lodge, Deepdene Avenue,
Dorking, Surrey, RH5 4AT, UK
www.templarco.co.uk

Copyright © 2015 Elina Ellis

First Edition

ISBN 978-1-78370-366-1

Edited by Alison Ritchie

Printed in China

BIG the Adventure

Elina Ellis

It was the start of a new day. Moose, Fox, Chicken and Bear stared out of the window and wondered what to do.

"Let's go beyond the hill and have a really BIG adventure," said Bear.

"A really **BIG** adventure needs a lot of planning and preparation," said Moose. They all agreed.

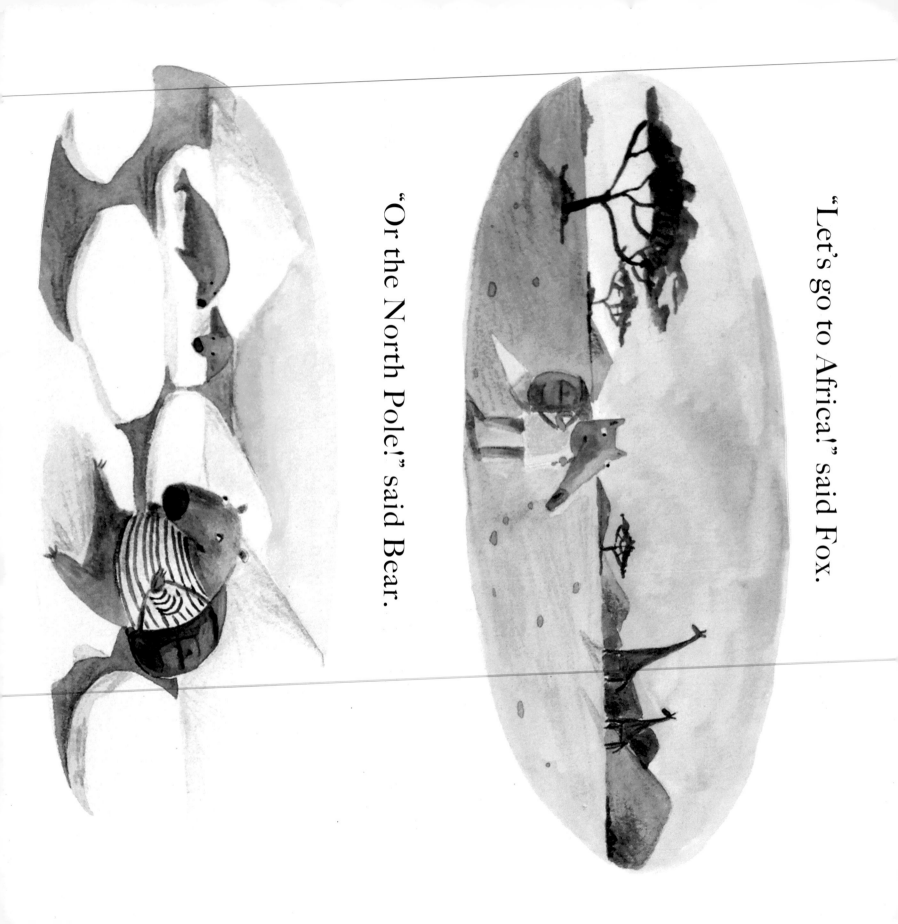

"Let's go to Africa!" said Fox.

"Or the North Pole!" said Bear.

"We could go to the moon," said Moose.

"Or to the next village," said Chicken. "My auntie lives there."

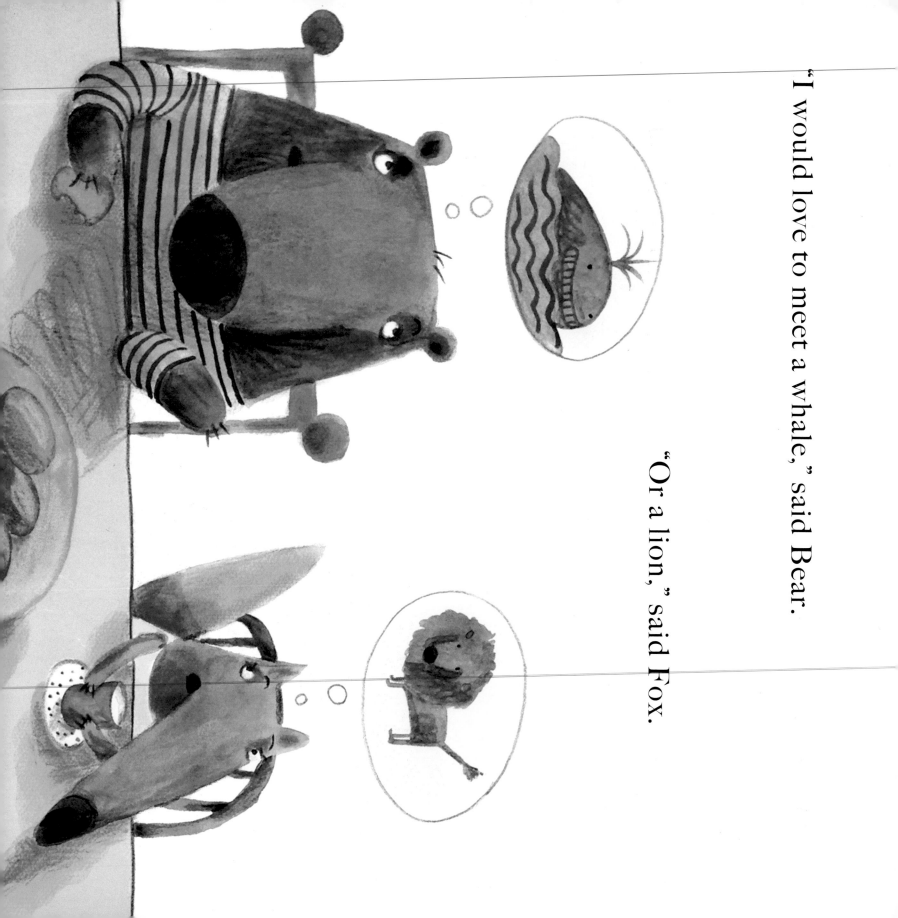

"I would love to meet a whale," said Bear.

"Or a lion," said Fox.

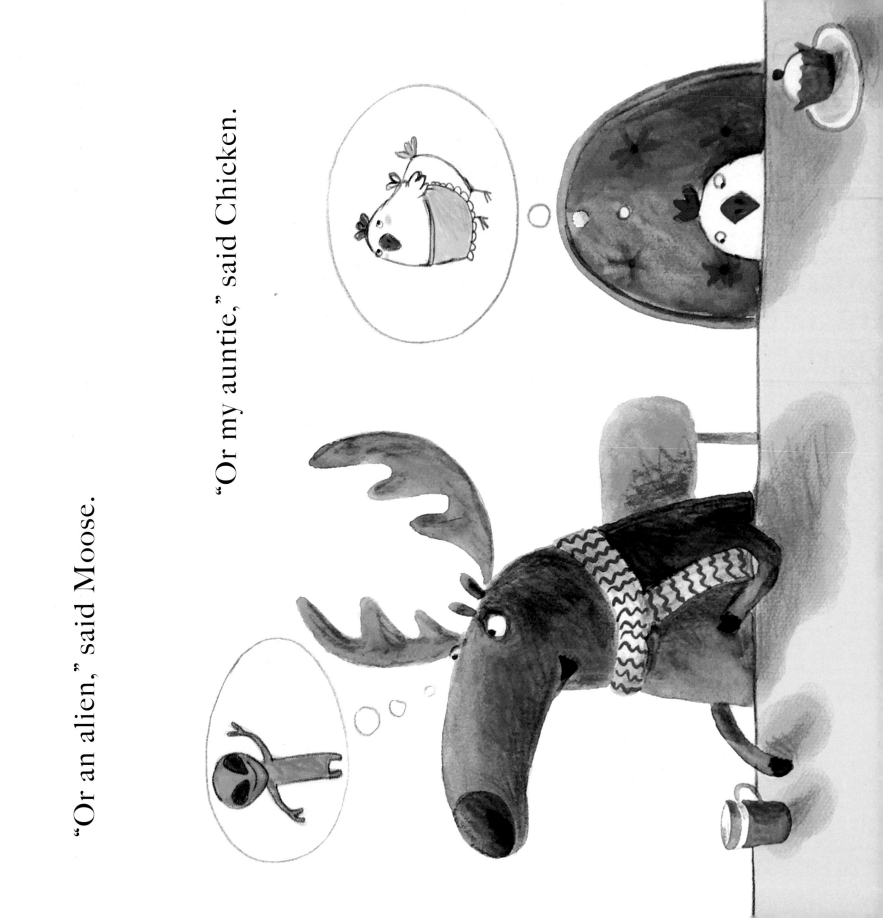

"Or an alien," said Moose.

"Or my auntie," said Chicken.

They started to pack.

"We'll need these," said Fox.

"And these," said Moose.

"And we can't go without these," said Bear.

"Are you sure?" asked Chicken.

Then they began to get anxious.
"What if there is a STORM?"
worried Moose.

"Or a fire?" shuddered Bear.

"Or a crash?" shivered Fox.

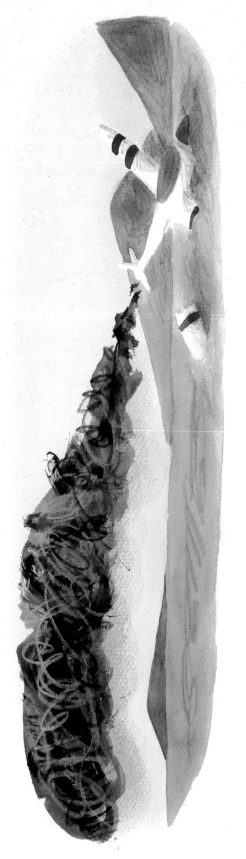

"There won't be," said Chicken.

The night before the **big adventure**, Moose, Fox and Bear lay wide awake.

"I can't sleep," said Moose.

"I'm scared," said Fox.

"My tummy feels funny," said Bear.

Chicken said nothing.

In the morning, the four friends
checked their map…

and climbed up the hill.

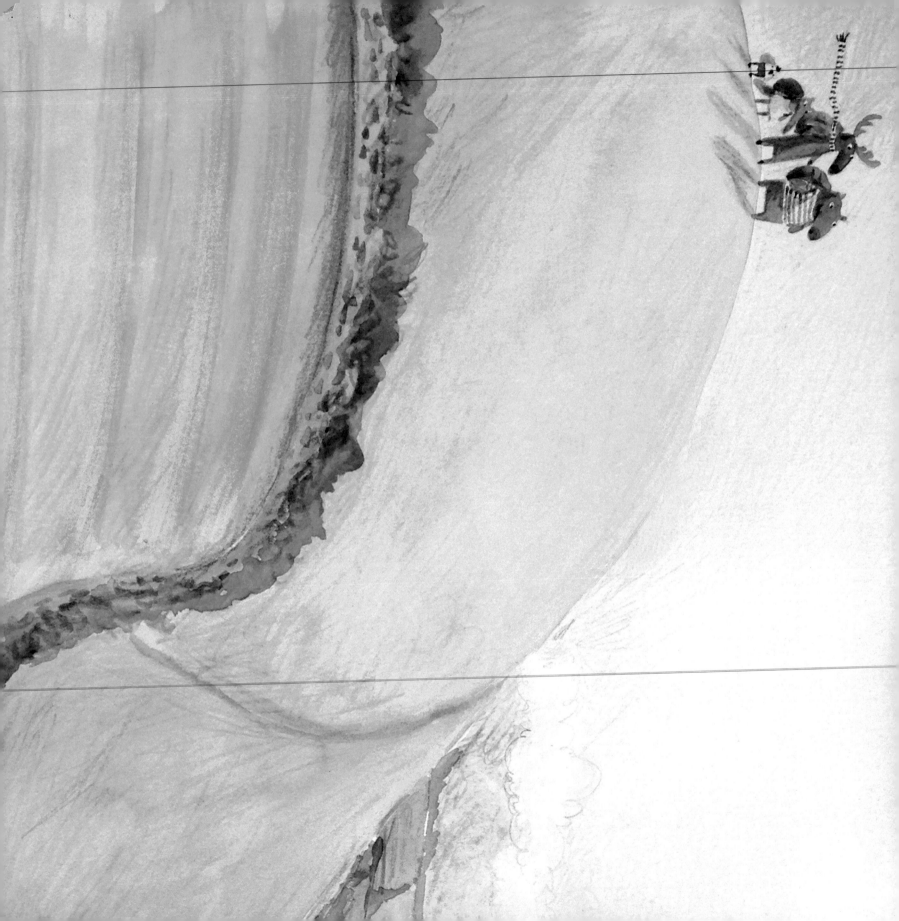

When they reached the top, they gazed around them. The other side of the hill looked beautiful!

And so did the little village where
Chicken's auntie lived.

"How far is it to Africa?" asked Fox.

"How about the North Pole?" asked Bear.

"And the moon?" asked Moose.

"They are a long, long way away," said Chicken.

"But the village where my auntie lives is right there!"

They ran down the hill towards the village.

"This isn't as scary as going to Africa," said Fox.

"Or as cold as going to the North Pole," said Bear.

"Or as far as the moon," said Moose.

"And if we hurry, we will be just in time
for tea with my auntie," said Chicken.

"This is the nicest adventure ever!" said Moose.
"And the tastiest!" added Fox.
"And not at ALL scary!" said Bear.

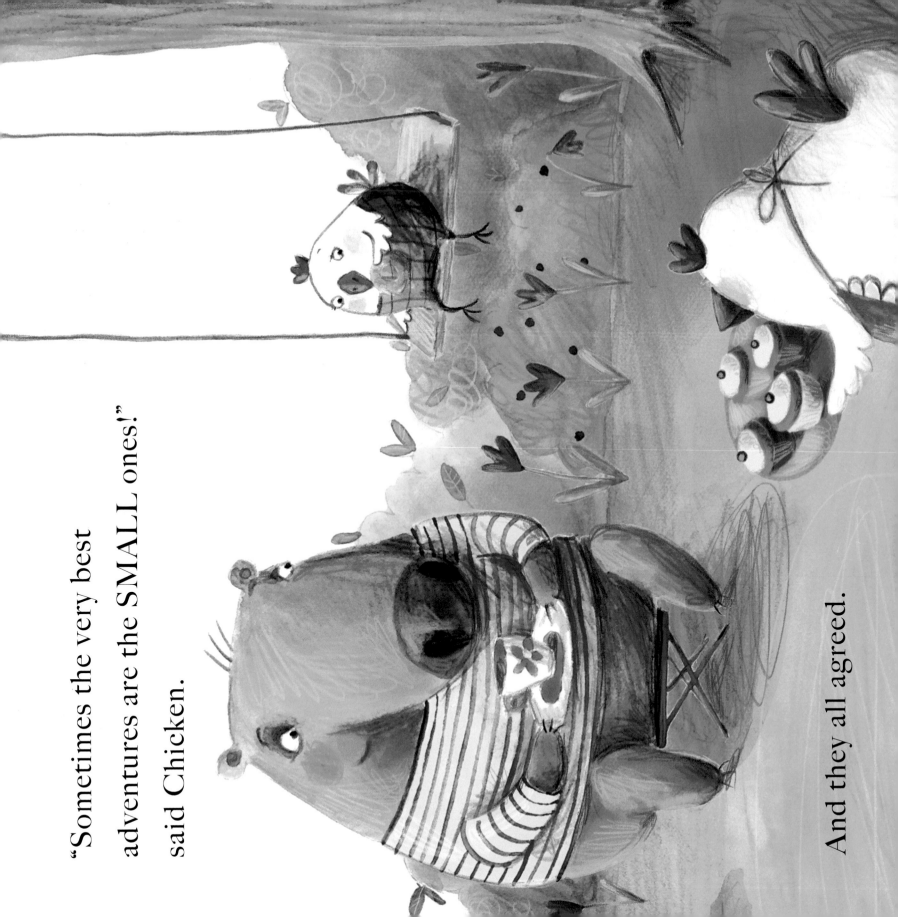

"Sometimes the very best adventures are the SMALL ones!" said Chicken.

And they all agreed.